Pawsatively Different

Remember to always be you and be kind

Written By Adam Snider
Illustrated by Cindy Sonians
Special Thanks to Kayla Hembree

Winnie and her friends, Remy and Cash

loved to spend time together playing, going

to the park, and swimming.

Cash was always full of energy and excited for the new day's activities. Remy was shy and hesitant to meet new dogs, but with the support of her friends has the confidence for anything!

One day, Winnie and her friends were at the park playing one of their favorite games, freeze tag.

While they were playing, Winnie noticed

someone playing by themselves in the sand

pit. Winnie stopped the game to tell her

friends what she saw.

Cash was so excited to meet someone new

that he started running in circles! But Remy

looked at the other dog and became

nervous.

"Let's go meet her, I can't wait!" Cash exclaimed. "But she only has three legs," Remy replied quietly. "What if other dogs look at us funny for playing with her? What if she can't play the games that we want to play?"

"It's not fair to judge someone by how they look," Winnie told them. "Let's go meet her!"

Remy understood that it was wrong to judge others but still felt very anxious about meeting a new dog. "But what if she doesn't like the games we play?" she said. "We won't know unless we go talk to her!"

Winnie replied. "It's a bad feeling when you are alone. They deserve someone to play with when they come to the park!"

Cash was so excited at the thought of

meeting a new friend, that he was still

spinning around in excitement. "Lets go talk

to her" exclaimed Cash. "Okay", Remy said.

"If you want to go talk to her, I will too.

Let's go."

Winnie, Remy, and Cash walked up to greet

the new dog. "Hey, I'm Winnie, and this is

Cash and Remy." The new dog looked

down timidly. "Hey"

"What's your name?" asked Winnie. The

new dog picked her head up slowly. "I'm

Elphie."

"Where are your friends? Why are you by yourself?" Remy asked. Elphie looked nervous when she answered. "We just moved here, and I don't have many friends yet. Most dogs don't want to play with me because I look different, and I can't play everything they want to."

"I usually just come to the park alone. I

want to make friends, but I don't know

how to. I get nervous talking to new dogs

because I'm scared they will judge me for

how I look or will not want to play", Elphie

explained.

"Well, do you want to play freeze tag?"

Cash asked excitedly. "No thanks," Elphie

responded. "I probably cannot run as fast as

you and don't want to slow you down or

ruin your game."

"Nonsense!" proclaimed Winnie. "We would love for you to play with us! We don't care how you look!" Then Cash yelled out, "I'M IT!" and they all start running.

After playing for a few minutes, Winnie

noticed that even though Elphie was playing

with them, she mostly stayed to the side

and wasn't looking very happy to be in the

game. "Are you okay?" she asked Elphie.

"Yes," Elphie said, "but you are so fast, and I can't keep up."

"We can play a different game!" Winnie said. "So we can all have fun!"

"You don't have to do that," Elphie responded. But Winnie was tired of freeze tag. She had a better idea!

Winnie ran over to Remy and Cash.

"We're going to play a new game!"

Cash jumped up eagerly. "What new

game?"

"Our new friend Elphie is going to pick!"

Elphie looked shy. "It's okay, I don't have to

pick. We can play tag again if you want."

"No, that's a great idea! You can decide

what we play!" Cash said.

"That way we can all have fun!" Remy

agreed.

Elphie looked at her new friends with a big

smile. "What if we hit the ball around to

each other?"

Elphie had so much fun playing ball with her

new friends. For the first time in a long

time, Elphie felt comfortable with who she

was. She knew she'd made friends today

who would not judge her and accepted her

exactly as she looked.

When the sun was going down and it was

time to go home, Elphie thanked Winnie,

Cash and Remy for playing.

"We're all friends now!" Winnie smiled.

"Whenever you want to play, we will

always be here for you!"

Elphie walked home with her new friends

as the sun set, happy and ready to play with

them again tomorrow.

GOOD BYE

www.ingramcontent.com/pod-product-compliance
Lightning Source LLC
Chambersburg PA
CBHW040928110726

48006CB00001B/106